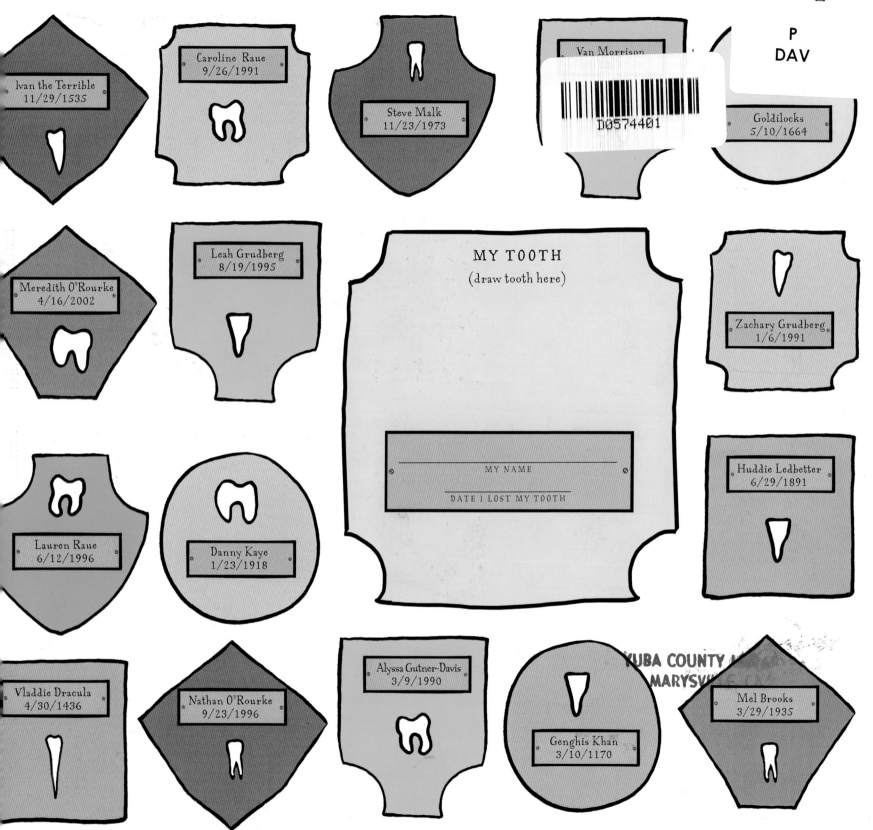

Ivan the Terrible
11/29/1535

Caroline Raue
9/26/1991

Steve Malk
11/23/1973

Van Morrison

P
DAV

Goldilocks
5/10/1664

Meredith O'Rourke
4/16/2002

Leah Grudberg
8/19/1995

MY TOOTH

(draw tooth here)

MY NAME

DATE I LOST MY TOOTH

Zachary Grudberg
1/6/1991

Lauren Raue
6/12/1996

Danny Kaye
1/23/1918

Huddie Ledbetter
6/29/1891

Vladdie Dracula
4/30/1436

Nathan O'Rourke
9/23/1996

Alyssa Gutner-Davis
3/9/1990

Genghis Khan
3/10/1170

Mel Brooks
3/29/1935

KATIE DAVIS

Mabel the Tooth Fairy

and How She Got Her Job

HARCOURT, INC.

Orlando   Austin   New York   San Diego   Toronto   London

www.HarcourtBooks.com

Library of Congress Cataloging-in-Publication Data
Davis, Katie (Katie l.)
Mabel the Tooth Fairy and how she got her job/by Katie Davis.
p. cm.
Summary: Relates how Mabel Becaharuvic's failure to brush or floss her own teeth turned her from an ordinary fairy into the Tooth Fairy.
[1. Tooth Fairy—Fiction. 2. Teeth—Fiction. 3. Humorous stories.] l. Title.
PZ7.D2944Mab 2003
[E]—dc21 2002011592
ISBN 0-15-216307-7

First edition
A C E G H F D B

Manufactured in China

The display type and text type were set in Aunt Mildred.
Color separations by Bright Arts Ltd., Hong Kong
Manufactured by South China Printing Company, Ltd., China
This book was printed on totally chlorine-free Enso Stora Matte paper.
Production supervision by Sandra Grebenar and Ginger Boyer
Designed by Linda Lockowitz

Any author would give her eyeteeth
for an editor like Michael Stearns.
I dedicate this book to him.
You may rinse and spit.

This is Mabel. Mabel Becaharuvic.
Mabel is 42,364½ years old.

Mabel is a tooth fairy. The first ever.

But she wasn't always a tooth fairy.

In the beginning, she was just a regular old fairy.

But she hated brushing her teeth,

and she hated flossing her teeth,

and she especially hated going to the dentist.

That was unfortunate, because after a while, her smile looked like this:

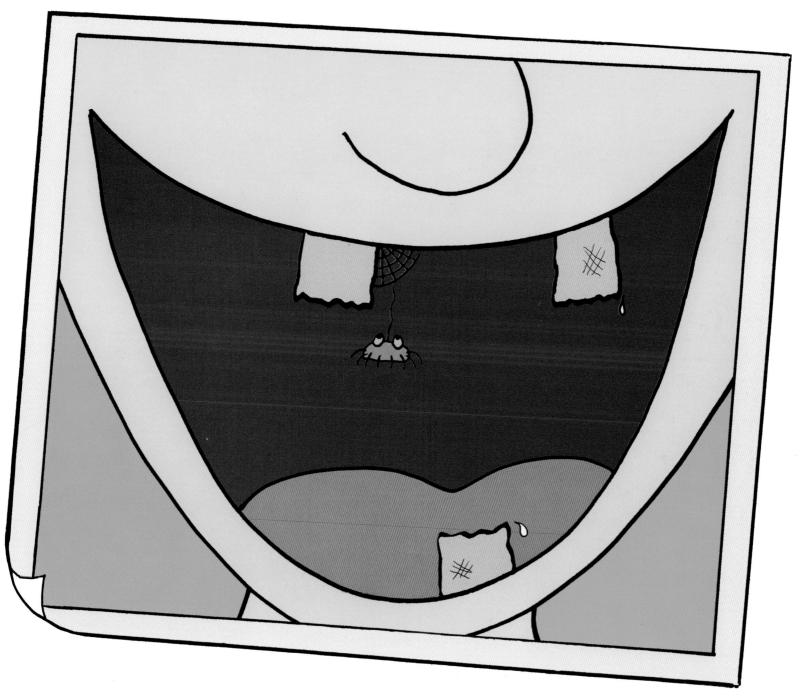

And you know, if you're a grown-up and you ruin your teeth,
they fall out of your head and you can never get them back. It was disGUSting.

It had a horrible effect on Mabel's social life.

But then Mabel had a great idea.
Kids lose teeth all the time!

She would take kids' teeth after they'd lost them
and fix up a whole new set for herself.

So that's how it all got started.

It was trickier than it first appeared.

She didn't want to scare any more kids
with her own dental problems, so Mabel decided to work nights.

Working in the dark presented its own challenges.

But Mabel thought the kids were worth it. She liked those toothless little children.

And they got to like her, too. Sometimes they even left her fan mail.

There were actually kids who WANTED their teeth to fall out so Mabel would visit.

After a while, Mabel had an impressive selection
of molars, bicuspids, canines, and lateral incisors.

But no matter how many teeth she tried, she never found the perfect fit.

So Mabel gave up.

She had no teeth and no friends and no reason to hang around.
Mabel needed a break.

The WikiWikiWacky Seaside Resort had a vacancy.

Mabel went beachcombing,

snorkeling...

...and played lots of tennis.

She got plenty of
exercise, but...

. . . she was still lonely.

Then one day, Mabel made a friend.

They had a lot in common.

They talked about halitosis, gingivitis, and false teeth every day.

But Mabel was really starting to miss those toothless little children.

And they were starting to miss her, too.

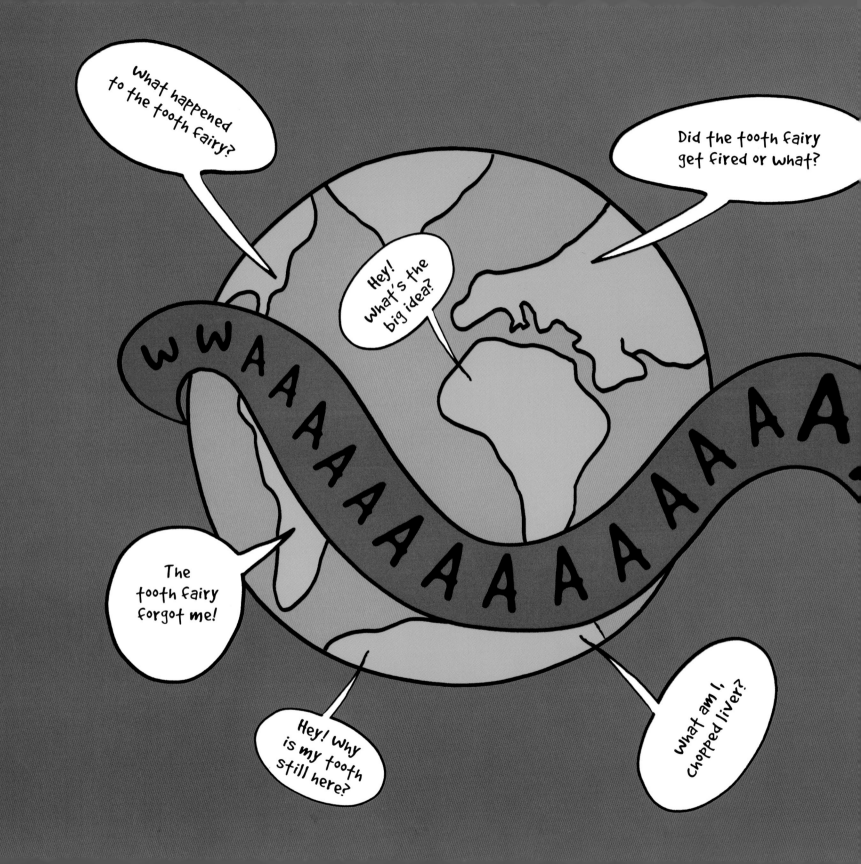

It was then Mabel knew that no matter how much she'd love to stay and talk plaque with Les, her heart was with the children.

She'd have to leave her only friend in the whole wide world and get back to work.

But then Les had a great idea. They could
still talk teeth every day …

…and Mabel could still visit the kids every night.

Now Mabel and Les work together.
He gives her comprehensive dental coverage and really nice floss.

But the best part of the deal for Mabel (*and* for the kids)...

...are the freebies.

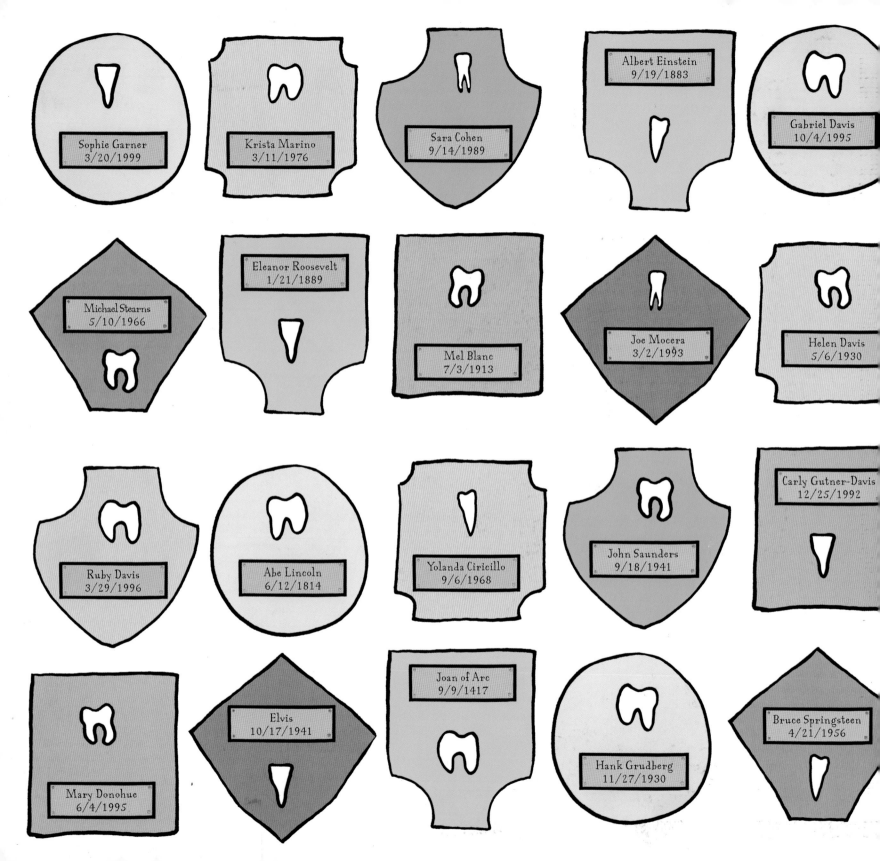